FATIMA WHITBREAD

MY BRIGHT SHINING STAR

Illustrated by
Rhian Wright

words&pictures

I live in a big house with lots of other children.

I used to live with my mommy. It was much quieter and I only had Teddy to play with.

Mommy sometimes found it hard to look after me, so Teddy and I went to live at the big house for a while.

When Teddy and I were taken to the big house, I made friends with the other children there. I guessed they were waiting for their mommies or daddies to come and collect them too.

"My mommy works late all the time," I said to Charlotte, as we played with Teddy and Panda.

"Mine too. . ." said Charlotte.

"My daddy had to move away for a while," said Tommy, popping his head out of the playhouse.

"I want my grandpa!" cried James.

Aunty Rae was my favorite of all the grown-ups who looked after us in the children's home.

"See that shining star?" said Aunty Rae on my first night, pointing at the brightest star in the sky. "That's the North Star. It always stays in the same spot, and shows you which way is north. Did you know that it can help people find their way if they're lost?"

I shared a room with Charlotte. Every night we looked out of the window together with Aunty Rae, to find the North Star.

Aunty Rae would then
tuck us in and sing to us
until we fell asleep.

North Star, North Star,
Are you near or are you far?
Shining with a twinkling glow,
Please show us which way to go.

One morning, there was a knock at the door.

I was so excited.
"It's our mommies! They've come back for us!"

"I knew it, I knew it!" squealed Charlotte.

"Slow down, my loves," said Aunty Rae. "You have to brush your teeth and get dressed first!"

When I got downstairs, Charlotte and James were gone. Their mommy and grandpa must have come to take them home.

Some of us stayed for a long time, and others stayed for a short time.

I felt sad whenever someone else's mommy came to collect them, but Aunty Rae always made me feel like I wasn't all alone.

"My love, there's a family out there waiting for you, and I bet they're looking at the same North Star as us. You'll find your way to them—the North Star will guide you. Till then, I'm right here with you."

Aunty Rae knew how to make me laugh.

Every day we had tickles
before I got out of bed.

She took me shopping and we'd zoom around the shops without even stopping.

Aunty Rae was strong, lifting all the bags. I helped with the lifting too, but sometimes Aunty Rae had to carry me when the walk was long.

Aunty Rae took us all to the park.

I played on the swings with other children who were there with their mommies and daddies—and I wondered when my new family would come for me.

One time, I saw some pretty wildflowers.

I picked them and hid them behind my back.

I gave them to Aunty Rae as a surprise.

I loved Aunty Rae and Aunty Rae loved me, but still I couldn't wait for the day when we were going to find me a new family.

Then one morning Aunty Rae told me that I was going to meet some families.

"You're going to spend a day with each of them," she said, "and at the end of the week you can tell me one great thing about each family. It's like a treasure hunt to find your forever family!"

First, I went to Andreas's house, where I had a huge, yummy breakfast. His family was big and noisy.

Andreas had three sisters, and everyone talked loudly so his grandpa could hear. Andreas's family was fun and there was always someone to play with.

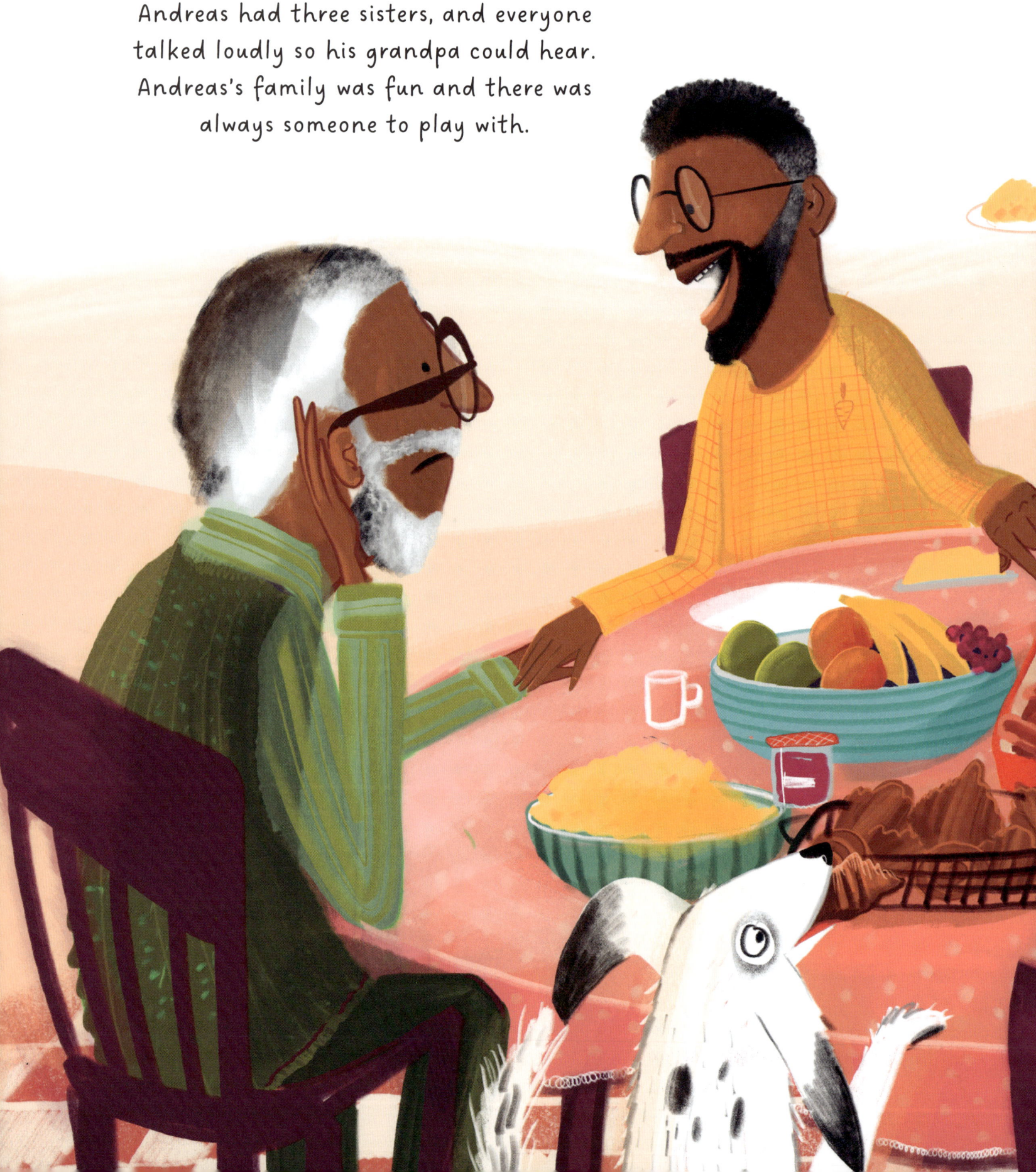

But it didn't feel like home to me.

The next day, Rene and Roberta took me to play in the park. They lived together nearby. They told me that they didn't have any children yet but they wanted to be mommies.

Rene and Roberta let me do the talking as we played on the swings...

and fed the ducks at the lake.

Then I visited Peter's family. He was adopted. Peter told me his mommy loved him, but she couldn't take care of him, so he went to live in a children's home, like me.

Peter's two dads knew he was meant to be their little boy when they visited the children's home.

Peter said his dad worked during the day and his papa worked at night, so he always had a dad at home to take care of him.

Peter had lots of toys and we had fun playing with them all.

But it didn't feel like home to me.

By the end of the week, I was so sleepy at bedtime. Aunty Rae tucked me into bed and said, "Tell me all about your week, my love."

I told her about the French toast at Andreas's...

and playing with his sisters...

I remembered the swings and ducks in Rene and Roberta's park...

and laughed about how I played the drums with Peter and all the noise we made.

Aunty Rae listened and smiled and held my hand. "Do you think you found your family?"

I thought about her question. Then I smiled and squeezed her hand. "Maybe not yet, Aunty Rae."

North Star, North Star,
Are you near or are you far?
Shining with a twinkling glow,
Please show us which way to go.

It had been a big week, and I had all sorts of feelings, but I knew that I would be okay because Aunty Rae was **my bright shining star.**

My Story

The one true constant in my early childhood was Aunty Rae. I lived in the foster care system for fourteen years and the most important lesson I learned from Aunty Rae was that in giving, you receive. Knowing this enabled me to live a relatively normal life in difficult circumstances.

Sports saved me at school. It taught me to believe in myself and be confident. Above all, it helped me feel free from my troubled childhood in foster care.

I met my adoptive mother, Margaret Whitbread, through sports. She was a coach and she nurtured my sporting prowess as a young fourteen-year-old girl at the local athletics club.

After a few visits and a two-week stay one summer in the Whitbreads' home, Margaret asked if I would like to become a member of her family. I had found my home.

I became an international javelin thrower under Margaret's guidance. We were all excited for the future. As mum and daughter, coach and athlete, Mum and I conquered the world.

Fatima with her adopted mother and brothers Gregg and Kirk

Aunty Rae encouraged me along the way. We always stayed in touch, and she was extremely proud of me. In caring for Little Fatima, in showing me that I was special to her, she taught me that kindness and love can make a little girl feel safe and strong. She was my bright shining star when I needed it most.

To Aunty Rae and Margaret Whitbread, "both" my shining stars.
My son Ryan Norman who has been my truest inspiration in life.
And Bertie my faithful hound.

"The brightest star in the sky is a beacon of hope, reminding us that even in our darkest moments, there is always a glimmer of hope."

Every child has the right to be happy, healthy, protected, and loved. - F.W.

For Nick, Elliott, and Eliza. —R.W.

© 2024 Quarto Publishing Group USA Inc.
Text © 2024 Fatima Whitbread
Illustrations © 2024 Rhian Wright

Fatima Whitbread has asserted her right to be identified as the author of this work. Rhian Wright has asserted her right to be identified as the illustrator of this work.

Copyeditor: Wendy Shakespeare
Project Editor: Alice Hobbs
Senior Designer: Sarah Chapman-Suire
Creative Director: Malena Stojić
Associate Publisher: Holly Willsher
Production Manager: Nikki Ingram

First published in 2024 by words & pictures, an imprint of The Quarto Group.
100 Cummings Center, Suite 265D Beverly, MA 01915, USA.
T (978) 282-9590 F (978) 283-2742
www.quarto.com

No part of this publication may be reproduced, stored in a retrieval system, or transmitted in any form or by any means, electronic, mechanical, photocopying, recording, or otherwise, without the prior permission of the publisher, nor be otherwise circulated in any form of binding or cover other than that in which it is published and without a similar condition being imposed on the subsequent purchaser.

All rights reserved.

A CIP record for this book is available from the Library of Congress.

ISBN: 978-0-7112-9624-4

Manufactured in Guangdong, China TT082024

9 8 7 6 5 4 3 2 1

FSC Paper | Supporting responsible forestry
FSC® C016973